Véronique's Jou

by

Patti Flinn

Véronique's Journey

ISBN: 979-8-9860600-1-9

Patti Flinn

Gilded Orange Books

P.O. Box 625

Blacklick, OH 43004

United States of America

https://gildedorangebooks.com

Prologue

Dear Journal,

My parents are worried.

At twenty-three they fear I will never marry. It is their most fervent dream that I find a husband, settle down, and have children. As a black-skinned woman—or a "blackamoor", as they like to call us—in a country that has few black people already, I couldn't be more of an outsider.

They would be thrilled to find a prospect for me.

I know their concern is justified. There aren't many men in France who would marry someone like me; a woman who's too educated for many common sans culottes *men yet too poor and common for most educated bourgeoisie men.*

I made the most difficult and important decision of my life. And now I'm here, writing sloppily with my quill and ink in the carriage on my way to a world I don't know, the ink threatening to topple over onto my clothes at any moment, and my fingers shaking with fear.

I'm being transported to the chateau of the highly esteemed Madame du Barry. I'm going to learn how to serve hospitably in the home of one who's been in the center of etiquette the world over. Jeanne du Barry, former mistress of a real king! I'm told visitors come from far and wide to appreciate her household.

It's a plum opportunity; unheard of for someone like me, the daughter of a freed black man from Saint Domingue and a free black woman born here in France. My parents love me unceasingly—that I know—but they vastly underestimated my desire to live my own life by trying to set me up with a man they should have known I could never marry.

The reality for me is that my choices are few. But still, they are mine.

I'm riding in this carriage to a new village because the events that happened during the past couple of months clarified my choices in a way that words never could.

—Véroniqu

Chapter One

The church was full but the three of us managed to find enough room to squeeze in together, my mother sandwiched between my father and me. Fortunately, our bodies so close together held off the late January cold that seeped in through the cracks of plaster and under the old wooden door.

My mother was a free black Frenchwoman who most likely had some aristocratic blood from down our family line because she and three generations before her had been teachers in the church.

Maman was a rare bird. The majority of the common people in France were illiterate but she taught me to read, and over the years had been working with Papa as well, but adults had much less patience than children eager to learn.

I looked around the small room to see if anyone new was attending.

"Always looking for new blood," my mother smiled, knowingly. "You know no one new ever comes to this town and no one ever leaves. Our roots grow too deep."

"No harm in hoping," I said. I sighed with disappointment as my eyes confirmed her words. No one new. And yet, the sooner I could find a husband the sooner I could get on with my life.

"Your friend is waving at you," said my papa, leaning across my mother. "Quickly acknowledge him so he'll stop making a fool of himself."

Across the room, close to the front, I saw Guy sitting beside his parents. He was, indeed, making a spectacle of himself, waving his hand to gain my attention.

Guy and I had grown up together like brother and sister, his house being the closest to ours. I helped him take out his first tooth, and he'd raced to get my mother when I climbed too high in a tree.

With his perpetually messy dark brown hair and white skin prone to blossom with red patches at any change of mood, Guy looked as if he were twelve even though he was twenty-three. He was easy to smile and make people laugh, even now drawing chuckles from the people sitting around him with his foolishness and enthusiasm over gaining my attention. At my responding smile and wave he dropped his hand, motioned with his two fingers that we would walk home together, later. I nodded.

"That is why you cannot find a husband, Chère," my father whispered to me, his term of endearment, Chère—*Dear*—taking the sting from his words. "The men think you are committed to a simpleton."

"Hush," my mother swatted him gently. "Guy's a good boy and you love him."

Papa merely grunted in response.

His was a common complaint but I didn't think Guy's presence had anything to do with my lack of suitors. I believed my skin color kept the other Caucasian men at bay. Young white men who'd expressed interest in me during my younger years, began to avoid my direct gaze when I came of marriageable age. I was certain they couldn't get over the "otherness" of me—too afraid to ask for my hand.

I knew that many white-skinned people in our country were worried about mixing of the races but I didn't think it would be an issue in our little town among people who had known me from a babe.

I'd been told I was very attractive. However, I felt my eyes were too large in my face, and I had a slightly crooked front tooth that sometimes caused me to speak with a small lisp. But my hair was thick, curly, and healthy. My skin was clear and brown like nutmeg—like my mother's—and my body was shapely with hips that I was told promised successful childbearing. These attributes brought attention, if not marriage proposals. And marriage proposals were all that mattered for a young Frenchwoman in 1788.

However, my father wasn't helping my cause. He did nothing to actively arrange a meeting with the parents of the young men of our town. Instead, he decided to find me a suitor from outside of town, making special trips to other communities where he'd heard more black people lived, telling me and my mother that he was traveling to purchase tools or supplies.

I knew he was out fishing; fishing for suitors for his only—aging—daughter.

We heard there were increasingly more formerly enslaved, black people coming to mainland France from places like my father's birthplace, the French colony of Saint Domingue. According to French law, even if a person left a French colony as a slave, they were free once they stepped foot on mainland soil.

There were some people in our town who whispered their concern about the increase of black people in France, even as they said that slavery was important

4

the French economy. Ironically, the more slaves were forced into labor on the lands and in the Americas, it seemed the more enslaved people escaped to find their way to mainland France. Thus, to my way of thinking, if racial mixing was truly a concern, France should have stopped forcing black people into slave labor.

Though white people seemed to see us everywhere there were still so few of us that Papa had to search. So, off he went on his horse, taking long travels to find me a husband while refusing to make any effort here in town. Not that it would matter. All the men of marriageable age were taken now, except for Guy. I didn't know how parents could raise a black child in a town of mostly white people and reduce that child's marriage options down to nothing.

I didn't think my father would have a problem with me marrying a white person if I was a son instead of a daughter. He held tightly to the sins of white men from his childhood but sins of the white women had escaped like water squeezed from a closed fist. As a daughter, I was considered my father's property. An adult son would have been considered his own person.

The world held different rules for men.

Though, I did know why he held such fear. Papa carried such pain from his childhood; pain I did not even want to think of.

He used to tell me stories of his childhood in Saint Dominque. Stories about his small hands sliced clean through while trying to harvest sharp crops. The morning-to-night unceasing work under the hot sun. The way black people were not allowed to speak or sing or communicate; having to do it in secret as if they were not people at all.

And the punishments. Punished for crying from pain. Punished for being sick. Punished for laughing. Punished for running. Punished for daring to be human beings. And, worst of all, watching as loved ones were sold and snatched away; or being the one taken from everyone they knew.

Slavery was a life sentence for no crime at all. I could not even imagine it so I tried not to judge him for his feelings or what this meant for me.

I used to tell my white childhood friends about these atrocities and they didn't believe me. Their parents had told them that slaves were happy to work and that they lived well. Or that they were people who needed discipline and structure. Everything they had been told allowed them not to have to think or question slavery at all. My father's first-hand experience was a truth they didn't want to believe and it was easy not to believe something you didn't *want* to believe. I stopped talking to them about it.

Papa told me about his love for his mother and brother and said that once he was free he considered staying on the island because the thought of leaving his family was almost too painful to contemplate. But there was always the possibility that another slave owner would again enslave him. His mother encouraged him to take his freedom and live a life she couldn't even dream of, that was how much she loved him.

So, he took the little he did have and came to France, where they spoke the language he already knew, and he was grateful that on the mainland he would forever be free. But though he escaped that life, the sadness never left him, knowing he would never see his mother or brother again. And he could never escape his mistrust of the skin color that held his family captive enough to willingly give his daughter's hand in marriage to a white-skinned man.

As for me, in our world, women in good homes did as they were told and followed their father's wishes to marry. So, my future was at his mercy. I was comforted by the fact that he loved me and would do his best for me. I didn't criticize his fishing even if I knew he was fishing for men who didn't want me at all ... he'd yet to find the right man who would understand me.

But he should have started sooner and gotten it done by now because with every passing day I was losing the desire to marry, at all.

The pastor began to speak but was interrupted as a former childhood friend of mine entered behind us, causing many of us to turn around and look. She was red-faced with embarrassment. Big with child and holding onto the hand of two small children on either side of her and sporting a freshly blackened eye. She held her chin up and hustled her babies into a seat as her husband came in behind her, his face a mask of arrogance, daring anyone to say anything. He took the seat beside his family, slouched in the chair like a pouting child.

I leaned to whisper to my mother, eyes still on the man. "He will beat or breed her to death. The bastard. When he was courting her he had nothing but fine words about how well he would treat her. Now she is stuck with him forever."

"Oui," Maman nodded, her pretty features turned down in a frown. "It is a shame. He is angry that he is a married man. If she had a little money put way she could send him on his way to do as he pleases, away from her, and find another man who would appreciate a decent woman in his home."

"But Maman, what you're proposing is a sin, isn't it?"

She blushed. "I never said she would have relations with another man, only that she could live with him as in a ... partnership of sorts."

I didn't respond though my lips quirked.

My former girlfriends were all married and had started making babies before the age of seventeen. And once they started having those babies they never seemed to stop coming, the church seeming to vibrate with the constant hum of babbling babies. I could only watch in amazement at the speed with which women of my age procreated, bringing new life as quickly as if they were in a race to see who could make more in the least amount of time.

"Maman," I whispered, my eyes on yet another full belly. "How is a woman able to stop having all those babies, if she wants to?"

"Hush! God would strike you down for trying to stop His will. However many babies you are graced with is the exact number of babies the Lord wants you to have. Now, make sure you take time to go to confession to ask God to forgive you for these thoughts."

My parents had wanted more children but had only been graced with me. As the years ticked by, I was sure they were wondering at God's will that they should not have grandchildren, either.

Chapter Two

"Where have you been?" Guy asked as we walked home after church. "I haven't seen you out much at all and you haven't come over for my mother's breakfast. She made crèpes just for you yesterday but you never came."

"Apologize to her for me," I said. "I haven't felt much like leaving the house. I started a new dress. Well, I started it in my head. The fabric I want is too expensive right now but maybe in a month or so I'll make something pretty for Maman."

Truly, the only thing that allowed time to pass quickly for me was my needlework. Just thinking about my new design made me want to smile.

"Is that the only reason you've been hiding?"

Guy knew me too well.

"I'm not hiding," I said. "I'm just exhausted from the constant talk about marriage. I used to have parents, now I have two matchmakers who can't tolerate the idea of a daughter without a husband. And every time I go into town I have to pretend not to hear everyone whispering about how I am wilting on the vine."

There were generally two groups of black people in France: the common laborers/servants and the wealthy. There weren't many in-between and the groups kept to their own. Papa was a laborer so he always sought out those he was familiar with, first. His fishing efforts had managed to snag some unsuspecting men on his hook.

The prospects he caught would come to our home expecting dinner, and then discover the hot meal came with a price – being forced to sit next to the unmarried daughter of the man they'd just met, looking like the fish out of water they were. Or a few would come fully aware of Papa's intentions, but expecting something different, it seemed, than what I was. All of them, after eating, would politely nod to me on their way out the door, never to be seen again.

Wealthy black men were a different story. Those men were, generally, either bourgeoisie (professional men like doctors or bankers), foreign sons of chieftains sent to France for advanced education, or the mixed-blood offspring of French colonial plantation owners and their female slaves. The latter group were called the gens-de-couleurs—*the people of color*—and were often sent to France either for education or to claim their family assets.

9

Papa stalked the wealthy men just as fervently as the non-wealthy one not imagining there was much difference in the way either group should b approached. He told us he had to be firm and fast with the wealthy ones becaus they were always in a rush and were short-tempered. Papa would run into thes men in town, convinced by their dress and their bearing that they were goo prospects, pitching my value to them like he was selling them a side of cow. loved my Papa, but I shuddered to think of how he presented the idea of me t those men in his desperation to marry me off.

I didn't know how many bourgeoisie men my father had approached but o one particular day, one showed up.

I was scrubbing vegetables and happened to glance out of our kitche window one day and saw a lovely, expensive carriage coming up the lane. I peere and saw a brown face from inside the window but its attention was on th property and not me. His eyes roved all around the grounds, and when he wa almost to our house the carriage stopped and turned around, as awkwardly a you would imagine for two poor horses to make a U-turn dragging an expensiv carriage with a full-grown driver and passenger.

I could only imagine that the worn stones and little farmhouse in need c repair told him all he needed to know about me and my station. My only comfo was that I didn't believe he saw my face. It would have felt even worse to b looked in the eye before seeing him turn tail to run away.

It felt horrible not to be chosen. Even if, sometimes, you didn't want th thing you were not being chosen for. Even if every day you wondered if marriag wasn't a trap to sucker women into. Chosen or not, feeling like a bruised piece c fruit at the market was demoralizing. Getting older and riper every day, but no a good kind of ripeness; the squishy, unpleasant stage just before being groun into food for the garden ripeness.

All of these thoughts about what had taken over our home was heavy on m mind as I walked beside Guy. He waited for me to continue; he was good lik that.

"I overheard my parents whispering in their room the other night," I finall told him. "My mother was saying: '...but Véronique can learn to work harde And then Papa said, '...she is a good girl and a hard worker for mainland Franc But the man told me that she is too soft. Not just her soft hands, but in he softness as a person. He tells me he can do nothing with a woman who likes t ew and read. She behaves like a wealthy woman but she is not wealthy. These men I bring are laborers. They say she is a girl-child, not a woman. A girl-child at wenty-three.'"

My eyes burned with humiliation and I rubbed a hand over them before they ould embarrass me by welling up with tears. I continued.

"Maman insisted I tended animals as well as any man but Papa said I could nly handle the easy animals and that he and Maman had done me a disservice y spoiling me. He called me spoiled. I've worked all my life and my father thinks 'm spoiled. I'm a disappointment to him!"

I'd been a servant—a *domestique*—since I was old enough to hold a duster. I iked the work because I was good at it. But my true love was creating beautiful lothes and dresses. I could sew a dress with stitches so fine and delicate you ould barely see where one piece of material ended, and another began. But my ruest talent was in the art of creating beautiful designs without a pattern. I did it n my head. And I loved doing it.

The only thing that held me back was the expensive material and fabric that could never afford. I saw it on noblewomen in town and practically salivated ver the fineness. I felt real silk once after taking the wrap of a woman and it took ll my self-control not to bury my face in it then and there.

Sewing was considered to be the work of laborers and the serving class. But titching for beauty and fun and the art of it–that was the pastime of women of eisure. It shouldn't have to be that way but it was. Add to that, the fact that I was ducated, and I might as well have been an even rarer bird than my mother. Rare r useless, depending upon how you looked at it.

Because I straddled both groups I belonged to neither.

"Véronique, you could never be a disappointment to your papa. He didn't nean it."

"He did. They made me what I am, the two of them, so how is this my fault? What's so bad about loving to sew?"

"And you love to listen to music when they play free in the square long past ime when everyone else has gone. And you love to read. You can spend hours eading."

"What's wrong with that?"

"Nothing! You're a dreamer, Véronique, that's all."

11

I thought about what I'd just seen in church and what I'd been seeing over the years. All my childhood girlfriends were married but, as the years rolled by, they weren't setting a good example for why I should be. Over the years I noticed how the men they married quickly lost the thrill of being husbands and began to get short with them. And the cheating. My Lord, how those men cheated. And drank. And cussed their wives out on Saturday only to show up in church on Sunday with faces wiped clean of the last night's devilment. Those men who seemed so enamored with the beauty of the first bloom of womanhood in their wives now didn't see the beauty in the maturity of womanhood. And they took it out on the women.

"I don't even want to be married if it means constant pregnancy and a black eye as a reward."

"Not all marriages are like that. You know my parents want me married, too. They're starting to worry that no one will have me. My father told me that I'm getting too old not to put down roots and start my own family. When they took me on at the cattle farm my father was happy because it pays better than what we earn on our little home farm. He took it to mean I was ready to marry. I think if I don't leave soon he'll kick me out. I told him to just build me a house on the land next to his – no need of both of us paying to rent the land. He got mad at me and said ... he said words... well, I think he wants me away from home. But I'm a man and I have more time. You know?" he said, licking his chapped lips. "Véronique, I will marry you if it will spare you from all the pestering. To help you out."

I looked at him. It wasn't the first time he had said it. I was starting to wonder if he secretly held feelings for me deeper than friendship, since he kept bringing it up.

"You're like a brother to me, Guy."

"Well, at least we like each other. Love each other, really. I wouldn't hit you and I'd try not to keep you pregnant, *constantly*. And it would get your papa off your back, oui?"

I gave him another look and he added... "He would get over the fact that I'm not black-skinned, eventually. He already likes me."

Guy's comment about not keeping me pregnant constantly told me he'd thought about lying with me and still had the stomach to suggest it. But the thought of lying with Guy made my skin crawl. He wasn't an unattractive man but he wasn't attractive to me in that way.

Papa did like Guy as the silly boy next door. Guy would be the last person my papa would consider, but part of me knew *he would consider him*. If the situation was dire—and it almost was—and Guy came to him and asked for my hand, respectfully, like a grown up. My papa would realize the young man he'd known all his life was making an effort and was probably the best I was going to get and then he would give Guy my hand. I saw it suddenly, clearly. Suddenly I felt my heart gallop a bit in panic.

If I married sweet Guy I would never be able to hurt him by leaving him. I would be with him for life and would have lost any chance to experience true romantic love. As much as I cared for him it was no better an option than those already before me.

Chapter Three

Leave me be!" I yelled. My voice was like a string jerking the nobleman's head up, his eyes wild with surprise at the sound. I could tell from the way he started he was accustomed to having free reign in quiet, dark places like this dry goods shed—free to do what he wanted to whomever he trapped. There was only one door and no windows—a perfect trap for a man with no morals and busy hands.

It wasn't the first time I'd been cornered by an undomesticated noble.

As a black female servant, I began my lessons in fighting off white male nobles before puberty. All women servants were prey but black women even more so. I was eleven the first time a lecherous man at a market stepped away from his wife and family, lay in wait, and jerked me into a quiet nook to fumble at my breasts. At the time, I managed to escape because I was small and wiry and stronger than I looked. I never told anyone, no matter how badly I'd been shaken.

Since then it had become a thing that, while not common, happened often enough that I was always on guard and usually had a plan of escape, be that an excuse for why I couldn't perform a task or a witness nearby to watch my back or at least provide a second set of eyes. This time, I had to go deeply into the shed. I knew the owner of the home was still away so I didn't give it a second thought. I hadn't considered his guest – a cousin traveling through town and staying at his house for a few nights. I had forgotten about the cousin completely until the very moment when I made to leave the storeroom, there the cousin was, blocking my way and coming at me with lips and hands.

"Shut your shouting!" he hissed at me, trying to pull me further into the room by my hips. The bowl I'd been carrying of dried beans fell, the little pellets scattering across the cold floor. "Be careful who you say no to," he said into my ear. "I can be your worst enemy. You don't want that, do you? Now stop fighting."

He put his hand over my mouth and pushed me against a wall. I opened my mouth wide, prepared to take a chunk of flesh from the palm of his hand, when suddenly his hand was gone and his body flung away from me. In the dim light, I saw the door was open, streaming light, and the figure in it turned towards my employer with his back to me to block him was none other than Guy.

"Don't touch her again," Guy said. Guy was an affable soul, not used to fighting. He wouldn't have known how to form a fist if his life depended on it.

But he adopted the best fighting stance he could. He stood with arms and leg spread, ready to dodge if the man tried to get around him. His cheeks were brigh red from emotion.

"Who are you? What are you doing on my family's property? Get out, now!

"I won't! I saw what you were doing. You cannot do that to Véronique, won't let you!"

In the dim light, the man's face changed from surprised to furious. H gestured to me. "He's a friend of yours, is he? You'll pay for this. Both of you wil pay." He pushed past Guy and ran out the door. I moved forward quickly to grab Guy's arm.

"What are you doing here?"

"I came to bring you lunch and heard you yell. Then I saw that man trying to..." he stopped, his face confused and dazed. "We must go find the law to repor him."

"Guy," I said as I took his arm and moved his face toward mine, willing the fevered fog from his eyes. "Listen to me. The law is coming but they won't come to protect me. That was a nobleman you grabbed, and you are on his property Whatever you say will be your word against his."

"And yours!"

"No better. It is our word against a nobleman. You must leave, now. Don't b caught here or they'll beat you first thing."

I bent down and picked up the bag, shoving it at him.

"Go! Go home! I will tell them what happened, but you must leave, now."

I pushed Guy a little, and that seemed to spur some sanity back into him. was glad to see him spare me a glance before he ran out the door and off int the trees to go home. I was still looking in his direction when a member of m employer's security team approached me. He was the combination grounds ma and security. We'd crossed paths countless times since I began working there a twelve years old and still disliked each other. And today he looked like he'd wo a lottery, he ran up on me so fast; his clothes still dusted with the morning' manure. But his grizzled face stared me down like I was the one that stank.

"The mistress of the house has called you inside the house to explain yoursel You've got some nerve attacking her cousin like that. I always knew you'd b trouble. I told them not to hire a blackamoor. Get inside."

VÉRONIQUE'S JOURNEY

I was scared, no lie. But fear never stopped me before. I squared my houlders, lifted my chin, and prepared to defend myself.

Chapter Four

The next several weeks were a whirlwind. After the incident in the shed, the law had visited both Guy's family and mine and we were told there would be a trial. Until then, neither of us was able to go to work, and being at home made Guy a little stir crazy. Guy was never one to handle stress well so when he was in town running errands for his mother and saw the nobleman in the street, he was unable to pass him by without calling him a name.

Rumor had it, the man turned to Guy and took his time calling him every name in the book that was synonymous with a piece of dirt. And then he took to calling Guy's mother the same.

Of course, he didn't even know Guy's mother but the insult was the point. This man knew he could say whatever he wanted and get away with it. Guy would have known the same. But Guy—being emotional—had pushed the man down in the middle of the street in front of no less than twenty witnesses.

I knew now it was so much worse than before. So yesterday I went to my former employer for mercy. I told him that I would work without pay for a month and Guy was willing to do recompense to the slight to his wife's cousin. The owner of the home, while loyal to his family, suspected I told the truth and was willing to accept my work without pay for a month. In return he would come forward to request leniency from the court on Guy's behalf.

Last night I trudged through the grass to Guy's house because now he was the one who wasn't coming out anymore. His mother appeared relieved to see me.

"Maybe you can talk sense into him, Véronique. He only ever listens to you anyway."

I found him out back patching up some stones that had fallen away with mortar.

"There you are," I said. "I have news." His mother, who had followed me out, watched us, hands on her hips.

"Good news, I hope?" she said.

"Very good news!" I made my voice brighter than the news deserved but I sensed some happiness was needed. "My employer believes my version of what happened. He will request leniency."

"For what in return?" Guy asked, not even bothering to look up.

I didn't like it when I couldn't see his eyes. He always looked at me when spoke.

"He's being reasonable. Just a little work without pay. I was thinking that yo might come tomorrow and offer the same."

"I'm not offering."

"Guy," his mother said, dropping her arms. "If it will help, why not? It something, isn't it?"

"It's nothing!" He threw down the rock he was holding and finally looke our way. Though he was obviously upset, his cheeks weren't flushed red fro emotion and his eyes were hard. "I don't trust the lot of them. If he believes yo why would he force you to work without pay at all? They'll have us working ou fingers to the bone and still throw me in prison. I'm not offering and neith should you, Véronique."

"You're being stubborn," I said, my happiness fading. "You're angry, but liste to reason. It's worth a try."

"No one else will give me work. No one. My reputation is destroyed. I had good job and now it's gone. My parents are being shunned in town because tha liar said I was trying to rob him. The damage is done. Now I'm supposed to be that man to tell the court I'm not a horrible person? I'm glad I pushed him dow I wish I'd killed him!"

"Guy!" His mother's hands flew to her mouth. "How could you say suc things? I didn't raise you like that. You're a Christian boy!"

He shook his head like he couldn't bear to look at his mother any longer.

"Give me a moment?" I asked her. "He's not himself. I'll talk to him."

She came over to give me a quick, hard hug. "You're a good girl." She kisse me on the head and went back inside the house. Guy continued piling stones.

"I know you're upset but this is all just temporary. We'll get through together," I said as he nodded back and touched the fingers of my hand. continued, encouraged. "I know you're angry about all this and I'm sorry abou that. But now you have to see the smartest thing for us to do is to go to m employer together. We can make a plan to work just for a little while. And the he will speak for you and we'll find you a new job, I promise."

"You're a dreamer, Véronique, that's what we love about you most. It's you best trait," he said. Though his lips smiled, his eyes were sad, which made me le

ncouraged by his words than I wanted to be. But his next words put my mind
at ease. "This is the only place I've ever wanted to be, but you're too good for this
place and the people in it. All right. It's fine, it really is."

"Tomorrow, you come by," I said firmly. "You get some sleep and things will
be clearer in the morning, you'll see. Okay?"

"Okay," he smiled. "D'Accord, Véronique."

**

The next morning I woke up feeling dread hanging over me like a sodden
fisherman's net. This chilly February morning, I tightened my headwrap and
went to the kitchen for a basket. Maman wasn't awake yet but at any moment
she would come downstairs, her brown skin shiny from being scrubbed. She
scrubbed it every day, faithfully, to keep the blood flow to her complexion. She
said it was her healthy brown skin that had attracted Papa when he first arrived
in France, a freed slave from Saint Domingue. "The way you get him, Chère, is
the way you will keep him," she told me, constantly. I was sure it was more than
her healthy skin that had attracted Papa to my mother.

She would be down soon to put on a pot of water so she could make the
hot, hot coffee that we all liked, with eggs and bacon and whatever fruit she had
found at the market that was fresh and ripe and cheap. We were very fortunate
that we could afford fruit. The eggs and bacon came from our own small livestock
farm. My father's knowledge of tending animals was the only reason we weren't
hungry, as were many in France. His work paid enough for the taxes on the house
and land we rented. My father had used two-years savings to build the house
with his own two hands after meeting my mother and deciding he loved her and
would put down roots in this town.

It was still so early the bright sun made the sky periwinkle purple and a layer
of early morning fog coated the ground so that I couldn't see the bottom of my
dress or my feet as I walked through the dewy grass to the barn to gather the
morning eggs for my mother.

The wooden door squeaked like it always did when I swung it open, like it
was pained. The purple sky was peeking through the gaps in the slats of wood. I
didn't need much light, I knew the barn by heart; knew where the animals were,
which animals were late sleepers, where to step, and where to avoid. So, when I

ran into a barrier it surprised me and I dropped the basket. But the barrier move
and when I reached out, it came slamming into me.

I went cold as I reached out again, shivering with fear as my hands touche
cloth.

The scream tore from me. I fell backwards and crab-walked out of the barn
the chickens squawked and the pigs snorted, and our horse whinnied in the dar.
I got to my feet and ran home. I ran and ran and ran. I never actually saw Gu
hanging from the rafters—my father spared me that by taking him down—but
didn't need to see it. I'd felt it.

Chapter Five

stopped doing everything I loved for over a month, including sewing and mbroidering. I went into deep depression, and finally, one evening when I rouldn't come to the table for dinner because I was more than full from a steady iet of tears, Maman came to me in my room.

"Asseyez-vous! *Get up!*" she demanded from the door.

I didn't move from where I was curled on the bed.

"There's no point," I said, voice muffled from wetness.

"Nonsense." She sat down on my bed next to me and pulled me up, despite he fact that I was a grown woman as heavy as she was. She managed to pull ie into her arms. "Chère," she said as she touched my hair softly with her hand. Véronique, you must get up. You must leave this room."

"Why?" I asked, looking into her kindness. "I want to die with him, Maman."

Her face lost its softness, then. She grabbed my arms and shook me a bit. Don't you ever say that, Véronique Clair. Never! I didn't raise you to say omething like that to me. Guy is gone and we are very sorry. He was a good boy nd he didn't deserve what was done to him but you are my baby. You being here nd Guy being gone are two separate things. Your death won't bring him back."

"But it was my fault, Maman," I breathed.

"No, it was the fault of that despicable man. He destroyed that boy's life with o more care than he would give a gnat flying round him in summertime. People ke that—that wealthy—they don't even see regular folks like us as human. You id nothing wrong, just as Guy did nothing wrong. He was good to you because t'aimait. *He loved you.* Like you would do the same for him. In heaven now, he oesn't blame you, Chère."

"He does blame me. He asked me to marry him, Maman. He asked a couple f times and I always managed to change the subject because it seemed a diculous thing to me. What if he truly felt that kind of love for me? What if by ot saying yes, after all that happened in that last month, I compounded his pain ll the more?"

She was quiet for a moment, absorbing that. "Your papa and I wondered hen he would get up the nerve to ask for real. Your papa would have approved nd then it would have been done."

She was right. If papa accepted for me his word would be it. That was the wa
things worked. Women often didn't agree with the choice their fathers made bu
they went along, besides. I would have married Guy if he'd asked my father fo
my hand.

"Papa would have approved?"

"Your papa has recognized he hasn't done well at finding you a match. H
grows weary and he blames himself. Guy was a safe choice. He knew he had onl
to go to your father, properly. But it sounds like Guy didn't want to be a saf
choice. He wanted to be *your* choice, because he loved you. He wouldn't hav
wanted you to be with him out of obligation."

She took my hands in hers. "I know you are feeling that you should have sai
yes. Who's to say if you had you wouldn't now be a widow? No matter what you
answer, you are not to blame for this. You are a woman now. I thought I ha
taught you, you cannot save someone who doesn't want to be saved. You did al
you could to help Guy. You tried all you could to heal him by loving him as yo
always have."

"But he came *here* to die," I said, looking into her eyes. I almost didn't wan
to say the words. "He knew it would be me to find him ... because he blames m
He wanted to punish me."

"Hush! Have you thought that perhaps he didn't want his parents to have t
find him like that?"

I hadn't thought about that at all—so besieged with guilt.

"Perhaps he felt safest to say goodbye where he knew you would be," sh
continued. "Guy had nothing but love in his heart. He didn't know hate even i
his pain. Don't disrespect his memory by making him into something he wasn'
He was just a sweet boy who didn't know how to get through this time. All of i
was too much for him. That will never change his love for you."

She took me in her arms and rocked me like a baby.

"I will tell you, Véronique, when you love a man you will take all his pai
upon yourself, if you can. That is what women do. It seems we are born lookin
for a someone whose pain we can take, even when we have plenty of our ow
And the world encourages us to do it. I can't tell you not to love. I only ask tha
you don't sacrifice yourself for a man who has given up. Go with him as far a
you can but it doesn't help any man for you to destroy yourself to save him. I
he's truly a good man, your sacrifice will only add to his pain. You honor him b

aving yourself. By saving yourself you save his dignity." She took my face in her hands. "Leave Guy his dignity. And you move on, my love. You go on with your life."

Chapter Six

'll admit, my mother's attitude seemed a bit cold and not at all like her normal warmth, but I did as she told me. With no reason to barter I cut my losses with my previous employer and sought out another job. I found I had been badmouthed to the extent that no one would even allow me an interview. Until, finally, Noblewoman Martin, an acquaintance of my mother, sent for me, asking me to visit her about a job as her live-in servant. My mother had met her husband and knew him to be a decent man. With them behind me, it would go a long way towards mending my reputation.

Two days later I stood in the parlor of Noblewoman Martin, my hands clasped before me and my parents' pleas to be honest and respectful ringing in my head, as if I could be anything but.

"Please," my mother had said to me, her skin pale with gravity. "You must make a good impression so she will hire you and protect you."

So here I stood, more afraid to disappoint my parents than the woman before me, my prospects for work in my hometown slim, and desperation rising with each passing day.

"I have heard good things about you, Véronique. You are the best seamstress in all of Burgundy, some say." Noblewoman Martin fingered the embroidered handkerchief I had brought as a sample. "Your work is impeccable. It is a shame that you had the unpleasant incident."

A streak of pain flowed through me . . . such clean words to describe what had happened at the shed and to the young man who had loved me enough to try to protect me.

"None of the noblewomen in town would be happy if I were to hire you," she said. Disappointment flooded me and I looked down. I could almost feel my parents' hopes and dreams die. I would never get work. I would live with them until they passed and then die alone with the chickens and ducks.

"I don't know if you realize," the noblewoman said, "I am not immune from scandal, myself. There was an incident related to my sister who ran off with the wrong married man. So, I understand how it feels to be tarnished by a bad reputation. It broke my parents' hearts, but my father was too powerful to be shunned. He was a banker, my father. It is amazing how much indebtedness can buy. People talked behind our backs and smiled in our faces. My father found a nobleman from far away and brought him here to marry me—a man wealthy and powerful enough on his own not to be so worried about his young wife's family reputation. I was very fortunate; God rest his soul. Thirty years my senior but he was a kind and selfless man, kinder than circumstances required. He never faulted me or made me feel I was any less than he. He saved me, and in doing so saved my family – brought us out of dishonor and reinstated our standing in society. But I think I will always feel like I have something to prove. My current husband is an equally wealthy man. I have secured my future, financially. And still, I never quite feel good enough."

I looked at her impassive face.

"Thank you, Madame Martin," I said. "For allowing me to present myself and my services. You are most respected by my family and me. My parents taught me from a child to disregard petty gossip. My mother has always said what a credit you are to Burgundy, giving to the poor orphans and donating supplies to the children even though you have none of your own. She has often remarked that you are a kind and gentle soul."

"Careful, Mademoiselle Clair. If you lay your praise too thick others are sure to think you are disingenuous or worse, mocking them."

I flushed. "I was only saying the truth, Madame, I would never mock you."

"Your mother is a lovely woman. And it was a small kindness to see you. gave her no guarantee of your employment."

"Of course, Madame," I said. I was anxious to leave. I'd had too many failed interviews not to know what one felt like. And yet she seemed determined to stretch the discomfort out.

"Did you do what they say? Did you lure the Duc to the shed so your male friend could rob him?"

"I did not," I bristled, though near to bursting for the opportunity to tell someone, anyone, my side. "If you want to know the truth, the Duc followed me to the dry goods shed and tried to take liberties with me. My friend only came to my defense because he heard my cry. Guy was a good man."

"Was? Past tense? Has he left you to clean up the mess he caused?"

My eyes prickled with tears that wanted to fall. "H-he took his own life. The damage to his reputation was more than he could bear."

"Oh, I see. I'm sorry, then. I suppose he might take his life if he was guilty, also, as easily as if he was innocent, if he's that sort. It's a shame he died without clearing his name. For his parents, and your sake. No church burial must have been quite a blow to his parents."

Suicide was considered a sin and no one from the church would speak over Guy's body, nor was he allowed to be buried in the village cemetery. Instead, we buried him on his parents' rented land and said our own words to try to set his soul to peace. But it had hurt not to have a Catholic burial.

"He needed to do nothing for my sake, he had already done more than enough by trying to save me. He was not guilty, nor was I. There is nothing a poor man can do to clear his name if a nobleman says otherwise. That is the world we live in and the reality he sought to escape. It is this world's loss to have sacrificed such a good and gentle soul."

Noblewoman Martin stared at me hard for a long moment.

"Your loyalty is commendable. What are your plans, Véronique?"

"Plans, Madame?"

"Yes. I overheard your mother once say that her greatest dream was for you to marry. She seemed to have a husband already picked out for you."

"My parents have tried over the years and would very much like to do that for me."

"Is marriage not an exciting prospect for you? It is difficult for an unmarried woman in these times, it would be prudent to marry."

"No, I have nothing against marrying, it is only . . . if I must, I would very much like to marry a man of my own choosing, Madame."

"Ah, I see. You young women today, so radical. Women can't have everything, Mademoiselle. But the one thing you *should* have is a husband. All else is secondary. Your mother knows that."

"I thank you very much for your time, Madame," I said. I had no desire for a lecture from yet another person. I was ready to leave and made a move to do so.

"I haven't excused you, Véronique. Will you insult me by cutting our conversation short?" She sipped her tea while I stood, growing impatient. I was grateful for the interview but I didn't take kindly to being talked down to. She put her cup down. "You will have a trial period of three months. You will be in charge of keeping house to include cleaning and laundry. You will not need to cook, I already have a competent cook on staff. You will learn how I like to do things and I will see if you fit in well. You will live here on premises. You should have no worries about my husband chasing you into the dry goods shed. Though you are exceptionally attractive, my husband is rarely in town and when he is he sleeps and smokes his cigars in the parlor. And he's not that sort. He will hardly rouse himself to chase you, or anyone, anywhere. You will move in and start tomorrow."

A blossom of light started in my chest and radiated outward. She was giving me a job. And I wouldn't let her down.

Chapter Seven

We celebrated that evening over roast chicken and potatoes. My father had taken to making a mash out of berries he found in the wooded area around our farm and we drank small sips of the sludge as if it were the finest wine. The next day I moved into the home of Noblewoman Martin and began my life again.

I worked harder than I needed to, to make sure she would never be sorry she had hired me. I cleaned harder, dusted items that didn't need dusting, beat the curtains with a stick when it was evident they hadn't been cleaned in years.

Noblewoman Martin didn't say much. She nodded a great deal at first. And, eventually, she relaxed to making small talk and asking about my parents. I didn't mind the minimalized conversation. I was happy to be left to do my work in peace.

Once a week on Sunday I would go home for dinner with my parents. I hadn't realized how much of a strain the scandal had been on them until the first time I came home for dinner and saw my mother's face had lost its pinched look. My father smiled widely at me and took me in his arms at the front door. I was welcomed into my family home like a long-lost guest and not the woman who had lived there a short time ago.

I was sitting at the dinner table scooping potato mash onto my plate one Sunday when we were interrupted by a pounding on the door. We didn't get many visitors in the country, so I looked in alarm at my parents. My father did not mirror my expression. He simply stood and walked to the door while my mother busied herself pouring tea into cups and setting down another plate beside me. I looked down at the plate and up at her in question when my father entered the kitchen. He was followed by a black man wearing a long coat rimmed in white and a cravat, holding a three-leaved hat in one hand with his other behind his back. He was tall, with dark brown skin. He nodded at my mother and I caught a glimpse of the thinning hair at his crown. He couldn't have been older than twenty-eight or nine, but he carried himself like a much older man. He looked at me, awkwardly.

"Mademoiselle," he said.

"For goodness sake, Véronique, will you put those potatoes on your plate and greet our guest?" my mother said, suddenly seeming nervous and giddy all at once. I put the potatoes on my plate, put the spoon back into the bowl and looked at the stranger, again.

"Hello, Monsieur. It seems my parents have neglected to tell me I would have a suitor today. And me looking a mess."

I did feel I was looking a mess. I had taken my headwrap off as soon as I arrived and my hair was loose about my head. I was still wearing my floor length work dress, and I was certain I smelled like the orange oil I had used to polish Madame's tables. But this man's face broke into a smile, his eyes still on my face.

"Not at all, Mademoiselle. I feel you are looking very, very lovely, indeed. As lovely as your father told me." He had the accent of people who came up from the south of France. He jumped a bit like he'd just remembered something and took the missing hand from behind his back to present flowers which he stepped forward on jerky steps to thrust at me. "Pour toi." *For you.*

It was a tiny bouquet of daisies. I accepted them, and he smiled proudly. "Thank you, Monsieur."

My mother immediately took them from me. "Please, sit, Monsieur," she said to him, gesturing to the seat beside me as she turned away to put the flowers in a small jelly jar. She could barely contain her happiness.

He sat beside me and fidgeted. Now up close, he seemed unable to meet my eyes. *Good,* I thought. I didn't want to see him, either.

Soon, my parents took their seats across from us at the little wooden table and we said a brief prayer. I could feel the visitor's eyes on my face as my gaze was lowered in prayer. At the abrupt end of our prayer I looked up to catch his gaze but he'd already moved it to his plate.

My mother knew how to cook well and, once again, I noticed one of our chickens had been sacrificed for this meal. That told me how important this man was. The last man they'd brought to meet me – a man of modest means who was the son of a man my father had met on his travels – had gotten a meal of root vegetables and corn meal pudding flavored with pig fat. But this man was being served the very precious breast of the bird, my mother carefully pulling a piece of crispy skin off the roast to lay atop his piece. She then carefully tipped the gravy bowl onto his plate, delivering a small pool of sauce made with fresh cream and butter she'd churned from our cow's milk.

He smiled, graciously, his eyes eager on his portion. "What a treat this is," he said, cutting into the tender meat and dragging it through the gravy like it was

quid gold. "I can't remember the last time I had such a special home-cooked
1eal."

"Certainly," my father nodded enthusiastically. He took the lower leg of the
ird and reached over to lay the thigh of the leg onto my plate. My father knew I
·ved the thigh even more than he did. My mother took a small piece of the other
reast. We, none of us, had as much fowl on our plates as the guest. "Monsieur
:ntier is from the south. His parents are both free blacks. His father has made a
ame for himself as a lawyer."

I looked at the visitor. "Really? A black lawyer?"

"Yes," he said. "As I am studying to be. I shall take my exams in a month and
1en follow in his footsteps. That's what I'm spending all my time doing these
1ys. Except for now, that is."

"Do you not work?" I asked.

"Not now," he said. "My father would like me to keep my focus on studying.
will work once I pass the exam."

I didn't press. His words confirmed that his family was wealthy enough
1at he could afford to simply go to school without worrying about finances.
[ost commoners had no education at all so, with his family having an advanced
lucation meant he was in esteemed status. My father noticed, also.

"You see," my father gestured to me with his fork and a smile. "He is a young
1an with a bright future. A wife of his will never want for anything. She can even
·end her time sewing pretty things, if she pleases."

"I have plans," the visitor said, the subject matter animating him more than
1ything had since he'd arrived. He looked at me and tripped over his words in
:citement. "My father is well known in the town where we live and while I could
so set up shop there, I could as easily go to another town to make my mark.
nagine, a bourgeoisie black attorney right here in town. I could be the first here
. Burgundy. It is only fitting to have a wife who is intelligent and educated and
:autiful, who knows the town well."

He went back to cutting his bird but I had frozen. I stared at him. My mother
1ickly picked up on my feelings. "We mustn't get ahead of ourselves. You are
1ly just meeting each other, no need to rush things."

The man looked at her. "...but Monsieur Clair said—"

"—what does it matter?" My father laughed and changed the subject.
Words mean nothing. We will all get to know each other, correct?"

33

My appetite fled. My father had clearly already begged this man to be my husband. It was more than a little insulting. I put my napkin down. "Excuse me"

"Véronique, where are you going?" Papa asked.

"Just a bit of air, I think."

"But..."

"Let her go," my mother cut him off. "She needs a bit of air. Let her have it and then she will come back and finish her meal. Oui?" She looked at me pointedly.

"Oui," I said. I left the room and walked outside to take a chair on the porch. The evening air felt good on my cheeks. Across the way the barn sat quiet and lonely and still. Beside me the front door opened and the visitor came through.

"Do you mind if I join you, Mademoiselle?"

I did the petty thing and did not respond but he sat on the seat beside mine anyway. "Don't be angry with me, Mademoiselle Véronique. In all our conversation your father never hinted that you were anything other than amenable to the idea of marriage with me. I ask only that you give me a chance."

I looked at his face. He was a serious man. His mouth not quick to smile. Stern to the point of looking like he would break, though that might have been nerves. I couldn't imagine why he should be nervous to speak to me.

"You seem like a very nice man," I embellished slightly. "Of course, I will give you a chance. And I ask that you give me one despite how rude I must seem to you now. It's my father I'm perturbed with, not you."

He visibly relaxed. "May we go back inside to finish eating. It has been a long time since I've had a good meal. The evening air is nice but it doesn't compare to your mother's cooking."

Laughter burst from me and I slid a look at him and stopped laughing when I realized he was serious. "Yes, of course. Do you have a first name, Monsieur Pentier?"

"Of course. I am Hubert."

"Hubert. That is nice."

"But you should continue to call me Monsieur Pentier. It is not proper for you to call me by my first name when we've only just met." He stood and put his arm out. "Shall we?"

And that was how I met the man who would court me over the next several weeks. He did lighten up, a bit. After three Sunday dinners, while walking of

nother meal of roast pork –we would have no farm animals at all, soon—he told
ie as we walked the path that it was now appropriate for me to call him Hubert.

I looked at him as we strolled, he with my arm tucked firmly into his, a hand
n top of mine to keep me there.

"I am glad to have passed whatever test allows me to call you by your name,"
teased.

"Propriety is important, Mademoiselle. If we are to be a respected couple in
ociety we must be beyond reproach to undo damage from the past and make
thers forget the ugliness from earlier this year."

I stopped there on the road, with the leaves swirling around in the dusky
ind. He stopped and looked at me. "Mademoiselle?"

"Is that what I am to you, then? A problem that needs to be solved. A lump
f clay to be molded into the woman you think I should be?"

"I didn't mean to insult..."

"There are many women in France ... if you wanted one who is spotless and
ure you should have found one."

"Are you saying you are not pure? Your father never said..."

That was when I turned, picked up my skirts and walked away from him.
he cold bit my cheeks and helped cure the fire in them. My eyes prickled with
umiliation and embarrassment. And anger. I walked into the house and went
pstairs to the place that used to be my room. I took my purse and turned around
) begin the walk to Madame's. Monsieur Pentier had planned to drive me in his
nall carriage after dinner but I was fully prepared to walk.

On my way out of the house I overheard my mother, father, and Pentier
)eaking furiously in the kitchen. I took the opportunity to leave, unhindered.

I had made my way down the lane and halfway to Madame's house when the
orse and carriage pulled up beside me.

"Mademoiselle Clair," he said to me from his perch on high. "Mademoiselle,
lease."

I kept walking resolutely, pride refusing to let me give in.

"Véronique." His voice was a plea and his use of my name an apology. I
opped. He reached out a hand and I took it along with his help onto the seat
ext to him.

"I am not a brood mare," I said, tightly. "But you size me up by my flaws and
eigh them against the cost of your reputation."

"You can hardly blame me for that. I am a respectable man ... when we marr I take your problems as my own."

"If."

"What?"

"*If* we marry. You said when. You should have said if."

He pulled on the reins and stopped the horse. Then he fully turned to m in the seat. "Mademoiselle Véronique, I know I am a stern man. I do not have charisma or an especially interesting way about me. I am simple. This week I tak my exam and when that is done I will be able to do the work my father and I hav always hoped I would do, someday. I want a wife but I don't intend to beg you. am a catch for any black woman. For one with a sullied reputation, of your clas I shouldn't need to tell you you are more in need of me than I am in need of you.

"You are right. You don't need to tell me anything. I know my station in lif And I've not heard anything from you that would suggest that beneath your clas and your charmed future there is anything of a human being about you. Tha is my problem with you, Monsieur Pentier. I am not a child. I understand th practicalities of life. But you ask me to agree to a lifetime of being nothing mor than a tally on a spreadsheet. You've shown not a bit of kindness or warmth. I'n no wilting violet but I am a human being."

I climbed down off the carriage and then pulled my purse off the seat. "I wi walk back to Madame's. Good day."

Chapter Eight

You must let us know who keeps house for you, Adele," said a woman who sat in Madame's parlor sipping coffee from a small cup. There were two guests sitting in chairs across from Madame. From behind, I recognized the chignon and the column of neck of Madame Doupe.

I had visited the woman four months earlier, respectfully requesting an interview, and she had stopped me at the door and called me a duplicitous blackamoor who would never set foot in her home. I was told to take my whorish ways away from her or she would call the law on me. As I left, she'd yelled at my back that she would tell all her friends to deny me work, and she had.

I had a pot of hot coffee in my hand, prepared to top off their cups, but on seeing her, I had an instant, bizarre fantasy of throwing it on her perfectly coiffed head. I quickly recovered my wits and turned away, hoping not to be seen.

"There she is, now. Véronique!" Madame Adele called out. I squared my shoulders before turning back and coming into the room. "Madame Doupe was just commenting on how exceptional your house services are, weren't you Madame?"

I stepped forward and the two women turned to watch me enter. Madame Doupe's face turned to stone when she saw me. I stepped forward, gingerly, to top off her cup wondering if she would toss the hot coffee into my face. I was hampered and slowed by the way she and I kept looking at each other, suspiciously.

"Weren't you, Madame Doupe, commenting on how wonderful Véronique keeps house?" Madame repeated, clearer and louder than before. Her guest's lips pinched but when I was pouring coffee into the woman's cup, she spoke in a stilted voice.

"Yes. It is surely a surprise."

Satisfaction blossomed pure and quickly. She might hate me but she would not lie in the face of her peers when the evidence was obvious before them.

"Thank you, Madame," I said, smugly.

I left the room then and overheard her say softly, "Are you quite certain you want to have a person of that sort in your house, Adele? A whore around your husband?"

"Are you suggesting my husband would behave inappropriately with the help, Madame? He would be disappointed you hold such a low opinion of him."

"No, Madame Adele, of course not. I only meant that you can't invite all sorts of people into your home. People of her sort, least of all."

I waited to hear Madame defend my honor, but instead, the other woman changed the subject and I was forgotten. But I did not forget the sleight. Later, stopped to see if she needed anything from me before turning in.

Madame was stitching embroidery by the fire. She glanced up. "Look Véronique, not as nice as yours but respectable, I think. Give me your opinion and do not spare me any criticism. I want to learn."

"It looks fine, Madame. I am preparing for bed unless you need anything."

She looked up at me and noticed my stiffness. "What's the matter?"

"Nothing, Madame."

"You overheard what Madame Doupe said, didn't you? You mustn't let words like that hurt your feelings."

"I've heard words like that before, Madame."

"Ah," she said, putting her work down on the table. "Then it is me you are upset with. You feel I should have spoken on your behalf."

My silence was my answer.

"I had already made my feelings known, Véronique, I saw no need to belabor the point. Just you being in my household is me speaking on your behalf. Did you remember when you interviewed with me and I told you that it was my first husband who bought my respectability? I could lose it just as easily by being too combative with the noblewomen of this town. I forced her to acknowledge your work. I will not put myself at odds with the women of Burgundy by shaming one of the most important members of our community to save your honor."

My cheeks stung with her words and what wasn't said. My friend had put himself on the line to save my honor and look what had happened to him.

"Of course, Madame," I said, picking up my skirts.

"Tomorrow after dinner we will have music in the salon. If your work is done you may join us to listen to it."

Chapter Nine

Monsieur Pentier sent word that he wasn't able to make the trip for the next two weeks and it was pleasant not to have to worry about being on my best behavior for Sunday dinner, and our farm animals got a two-week reprieve. Three Sundays later he returned with a more relaxed and dignified demeanor. Upon entering our house he looked at me and took my hand to kiss the back of it. "Mademoiselle Clair."

My father was near to bursting with excitement, ushering him in and making sure we all sat down and had said prayers before he looked at our guest, expectantly.

"Well, young man? Have you news?"

Hubert dabbed at his mouth with his napkin but could not contain the smile of triumph. "I do, indeed. I have passed my exams and will carry on my father's profession. I will be an attorney."

My parents' exclamations of excitement filled the room. While my father was jabbering on about future plans and my mother got up to rustle through the kitchen for my father's jar of mash, our guest looked at me, slyly.

"You see, Mademoiselle, I will be able to secure a fine future for you, if you should decide to be my wife."

I warmed a bit at his obvious effort to undo the damage he had done. He wasn't such a bad man, after all, I thought.

"We have no black attorneys in Burgundy and very few black families," my father said, thoughtfully. "If you move here, how will you support yourself?"

"Why, I will not limit myself to black clients, Monsieur. I will take any paying client."

"But will they take you?" my father asked, his brow furrowing. It was an honest question coming from a man who had been enslaved by white people most of his life. But he'd told me Hubert Pentier's family had always been free, as had my mother's. It was difficult for my father sometimes to reconcile the life he'd known in the colonies to these people on the mainland where black people were few and far between; considered an oddity but not hated purely for our color's sake.

"Not all, but enough to keep me in work, I'm sure," Pentier said withou doubt. "My father does very well for himself. And it's all about who you serve. will seek out the wealthiest nobles so I will need fewer clients. I'll make mysel known and trusted. But I can do that in any village in France."

"That's very exciting, Monsieur Pentier," my mother said, pouring him a tin bit of the sacred liquid in a glass the size of a thumbnail. "You might even end u in Paris, one day."

"It's, entirely possible," he took a sip. "What Frenchman does not want to en up in Paris?"

"But you'd be willing to live elsewhere, then?" I asked.

The three of them stopped at the sound of my voice, as it was the first time had spoken since he'd arrived.

"Absolutely. I'm very willing to consider any location, Mademoiselle. Do yo have one in mind?"

My parents smiled, affectionately, but my mother spoke. "Véronique has on place and one place only she would like to go. Ever since we visited some friend in Crossy-Sur-Seine many years ago. She fell in love with a house along the bank of the Seine, near where the jagged edges meet."

I was a little girl when we visited the family in the sleepy town. The road were quiet and a layer of peacefulness lay over the town. It wasn't a farmin community like the one I grew up in, but it was a working community. M father's friend's daughter had taken me for a walk through the neighborhood an there, in the evening dusk, we'd seen a tiny house with windows lit from withir It had warmed my heart. And when she led me further into the area around i I understood the strong sense I had of water nearby. Behind the house, a shor pace away, was ground that declined into the Seine River. I had looked at th slow-moving water, looked at the moon rising as the sun descended and was i love.

I talked so much about the beautiful little house on our day-long trip bac to Burgundy, my parents had gotten tired of hearing it. And then I told Gu all about the house. He'd decided then and there to move to Crossy-Sur-Sein along with me, as soon as we'd both saved enough money to go. That had neve happened but that was part of the reason why I worked, to save the money.

"Crossy-Sur-Seine?" Hubert said, his brow furrowing a bit. "Not much goin on there, is it? Though it's not terribly far from Paris, I suppose."

"It's a lovely little house. I still have the address."

My eyes must have been shining with excitement because he quickly changed is tune. "I know a man in the town next to it. I can find out about this house f yours. Though if it's been years I'm sure it is already housing a family and npossible to buy."

"Perhaps," I said. "But if you could check I would be most appreciative."

"Of course, Mademoiselle."

I smiled and cut into my vegetables. "Mother, will you tell Monsieur Pentier 1at it is perfectly appropriate for him to call me by my first name so that I may all him by his? He said we could but he seems resistant to actually doing it."

Hubert blushed and dug into his food as my mother smiled at my sass.

"In any other circumstance I would tell you to mind your manners, but she ; right, Monsieur. I feel you have known each other long enough to skip the ormality. Don't you agree, Chèr?" she asked my father.

My father smiled and nodded. "I certainly do."

Chapter Ten

The next week at dinner Hubert explained that he did, indeed, look into the status of house and found that it was empty and had been for some time. The owner had moved out of the country and simply hadn't taken the time to do anything with it. The floors creaked and the roof needed repair. The windows were so old they took in drafts during the winter from the cold air off the water of the Seine. "Two hundred lira he will sell it and be done with it."

"Two hundred lira? That's a fair price. And those repairs are little things that can all be fixed," I said at the table, chewing Maman's tender asparagus smothered in roasted garlic-scented cream sauce. "Minor inconveniences for someone who knows how to do a little work."

"I am sorry to say I don't know how to do any of that work and I wouldn't want to pay for it for that shack of a house," Hubert sniffed.

"Oh, that's alright, I meant me. I take care of chores around here all the time," said.

"She tells the truth," my father said, proudly. "My Véronique is a worker."

I felt a flush of pleasure. I might not be able to lift a cow on my own but at least Papa could acknowledge my work ethic. Only my mother's eyes, shifting to Hubert, seemed to hold some other thought. "Véronique, I think you will not be doing that type of work when you are a proper lady in your own home."

My father and I looked at her and it dawned on me what she meant. I would be like one of those ladies who sits in the house being proper. I would be like Madame Martin, spending the day looking at flowers and reading and being terribly busy doing nothing. As much as I loved to read, I'd never known a life without working.

It occurred to me that this was why people of different social groups didn't mix. The change in lifestyle was too drastic. But I also knew that in these times, in 1788, women did what their husbands expected. We would live as he wanted, not as I did. But, perhaps, his kindness and patience would make the change in lifestyle palatable.

I fell quiet, but later Hubert brought up the subject of the little house again.

"I know you are interested in this place you speak of but, practically speaking, we should set up house here in town. You will need the help of your mother for the children."

We were strolling the grounds of our farm after dinner. The trees were budding with the bounty of spring, all topped with varying shades of pinks, purples and green. Barely a breeze with slightly cool air made it a lovely night for a walk but he immediately managed to ruin the mood. I saw then that he only paid attention to my needs in the presence of my parents.

"Surely we won't start with children immediately," I said. "Maybe in a couple of years after we have put some money away."

"I will have all the money we need. My father will help us buy a house or build something modest. Something closer to the heart of town. Your parents home is lovely but it is a farm. A nice farm, but for our standing we will need something more palatial, befitting our place in society."

Society. I was growing sick of a word that had the power to create or destroy human beings.

"I don't need much," I said. "I'd rather have something modest and manageable for my own. I'm sure my parents would let us stay here until we can afford it."

"Here," his face told the tale. "I am a grown man and I will not live under the roof of another grown man once married. We will use the gift my father has committed to giving us when—if—we marry to buy our first home and start a family immediately. We will stay close enough for your mother to help you."

He was a grown man who wouldn't live under the roof of another grown man but he would accept a cash gift from one. I found a little hypocrisy in that.

"But I want to continue working."

"Working? Whatever for?"

"I enjoy working. And I enjoy making my own money."

"It is a sign of your station in life that you will never have to work, I will provide for you as a man should."

I didn't respond and he took my hand.

"It is clear society means little to you, but it is the way of getting ahead in life. Your parents are good, honest people. But your father tells me it has been difficult for you, at times. He wishes he could have given you nice things."

"My parents have given me all I ever wanted or needed. But my future is mine."

"I want it to be ours. I will make you happy, Véronique."

Chapter Eleven

On the Saturday of the following week I noticed a woman in the kitchen at Madame Martin's house speaking with the cook. The woman wore modest worker clothes like mine so I knew she wasn't a guest. Perhaps a cook's apprentice. I went about my business.

The next day the mystery was solved when I returned from my parents' home to Madame Martin's after Sunday dinner. I had only just come in that evening when Madame Martin called out to me on my way to my room.

"Véronique, come in here, please."

I stepped into the parlor.

"Please sit," she gestured. "I know Sunday evenings are yours but I have a matter to speak to you about that shouldn't wait."

I couldn't imagine what she wanted to speak about and hoped I wasn't in trouble. "Have I done something wrong? I assure you, I will try harder to fix anything I might have caused."

"Goodness, Véronique, are you so used to bad news that you jump to the worst possible conclusion? You've done nothing wrong. On the contrary, you've done everything very well, indeed. Your probation was over a month ago and I couldn't be happier with your progress."

I was relieved to hear it and happy that I had redeemed myself professionally. But it made me wonder.

"I saw someone speaking with the cook yesterday, is she a new worker?"

"Yes, that is Lisette. She will be shadowing you this week."

I couldn't hide my dismay. I liked running the household my way. I liked doing things the way I liked to do them. "But Madame, there is no need. I am happy and more than capable of handling the matters of the house. Another person will only be in my way."

"That's what I want to speak to you about. You might have noticed my husband's carriage out front?"

I barely saw her husband, thankfully, and when I did he was just as eager to be away from me as I from him. Then he would disappear into the study or his bedroom until his next trip. It seemed hardly a marriage but who was I to judge? It seemed to work for them.

"He's just returned from his first visit to the Palace of Versailles as an actual guest."

"An invitation to Versailles? Your husband must be very important."

"He is, but not like it would seem. He was invited by a nobleman who lived in Versailles, not the king himself, though he did have a chance to meet both the king and the queen. It was the highlight of his life. He said the palace is beautiful beyond words. He stayed for a full day and he is impressed with the way the palace is run. He said the serving staff anticipated his every need. He felt like the king himself."

"I would expect no less from the home of our king and queen," I said.

"They have a staff of hundreds. But my husband is obsessed with the idea of replicating that level of service here, in our home."

"I see. I'm sure I could handle it if he will give me a list of the services provided. Perhaps I can use the new woman to assist me."

"He could not give you a list because my husband, like many men, does not have the slightest concept of all that is done for him to make his life easier. He only knows that he felt cared for in a way he never has elsewhere. But now he wants guests to our home to have that same feeling here. Burgundy is no Versailles, but it occurs to him that we can make our home the Versailles of Burgundy."

"That is an ambitious goal."

"And it brings me to you. I am not of high enough nobility to request an audience at Versailles but there is another option. The Madame Jeanne du Barry was the mistress of King Louis XV, God rest his soul. At one time she was in charge of Versailles as if she were the queen, herself. She understands how to hire people who can cater to a king—in ways beyond the obvious—and I've heard she has transferred that knowledge to her staff at the Chateau de Louveciennes. In fact, Louis XVI allowed her to take many of the staff from Versailles with her to set up her home. Rumor has it, though small and intimate in comparison to the Palace, the Chateau at Louveciennes holds even better parties than Versailles. The Queen's own brother, the Holy Roman Emperor, chose to stay with the Madame instead of with his own sister at Versailles when he came to France. Nobles flock from all over the country to visit the du Barry chateau and leave feeling as if embraced by a warm hug. And she allows nobles to send their staff

48

o her residence to be trained in the ways of exceptional service. I've requested
ermission to send you."

"Me?" Excitement came quickly as I imagined learning how to be best at my
ob. Even more importantly, I imagined the wealth of noblemen and women I
might meet as potential customers. I could show off my sewing to people who
ould afford to pay me for my skill. I could get a foot in the door to become the
naster seamstress I wanted to be. I licked my lips, my eyes wide and eager. "You
re saying you would send me? Really?"

"Of course, I've already been granted permission. Look, here is the letter."
he picked up a sheet of fine, folded paper from the table beside her chair and
anded it to me.

It was a letter from the Comtesse Jeanne du Barry, official titled mistress of
he previous king. The penmanship was exquisite, and the ink was high quality.
wrote letters all the time but my handwriting didn't look like the letter in
ny hands. The way Madame Martin held the paper gingerly between her index
ngers and thumbs, I was sure the letter would soon be framed and hung on a
all. In that letter I read the words...

*...Yes, please send your servant, Véronique. We have a place for her. I shall
expect to see her at the start of the month. Upon arrival, my manager,
Gaspard, will direct her to her quarters. She will work with the head
laundress, help with whatever my cook Salanave should need, and she
can always go to my personal page, whom we affectionately call the
Governor of Louveciennes, Louis-Benoit Zamor, for guidance.*

*We look forward to meeting Véronique Clair and training her in the
ways of exceptional service. As you know, our dear deceased King Louis
XV—the Well Beloved—treated me with the tenderness of a wife and
trusted me to take care of Versailles. I bring those same skills to the home
we once shared and welcome all to the Chateau du Barry.*

Sincerely,
Comtesse Jeanne du Barry,
Mâitresse-en-titre to our
dear, deceased King Louis XV,

My mind raced. I didn't know much about the Madame du Barry, but sh certainly might have needed a dress. Wouldn't it be something if I could in on year gather a client base for a lifetime? I could hardly contain my excitement.

"So now it is time for me to ask you if you'd like to go," my benefactres continued. "The young woman you saw in the kitchen will shadow you ove the next two weeks to learn all she can before you leave for Louveciennes. O if you decline, I will send her instead. You see, it is up to you. I don't have t tell you how special it will look for you to be able to say you were trained a Louveciennes. It would wipe out any difficulty you have had getting a job. Ther wouldn't be a home in Burgundy—or anywhere, for that matter—that wouldn' clamor for your services at an advanced rate, though I would expect you to b loyal to me as long as needed."

The enormity of the opportunity was overwhelming. She was handing m the means to learn skills that would set me up for life.

"How long?"

"I have requested a one-year apprenticeship. Is that a problem?"

It wasn't for me but I wasn't sure how Hubert would feel. "It is only that m parents have arranged a possible marital union for me. The gentleman doesn' want me to work."

"I see. Does he want you to have babies right away, then? I have to say, I wa never blessed and at this point in my life I'm not sorry. But I imagine you wan babies?"

"Yes. Someday."

"I see. I can't tell you what to do. I can only tell you I will be sending someon to Louveciennes in two weeks. I would like for it to be you. Let me know wha you decide."

How could I let her know when I didn't know what do to? The followin Sunday I went home and before Hubert arrived, I spoke to my mother and tol her about my opportunity.

"How nice," she said. While her words relayed happiness for me, she wa measured in her pleasure. "Perhaps you should let it pass this time. Surely othe chances will come along."

"I thought you'd be happy for me," I said, helping her to peel potatoes.

"I am happy and very proud of you, Chère, but you have a much more ressing issue. The man who is courting you does not want you to work."

"Money is freedom, Maman," I told her. "You told me that. And you told me ork is a good thing."

"I still believe that, but you will soon be working hard to make the babies our husband wants."

"But I enjoy working. And I can put money away for the future."

"Véronique, you are the daughter of working people, so yes, we taught you o work. But we never dreamed you would be able to marry a man who can earn nough that you don't have to work. To elevate to an entirely different class is nheard of; it is a dream come true, Chère. And your father – to be born enslaved ad to live to see his child live a life of luxury ... it is astounding, ma petite. ou have made him so proud. And look at you. Intelligent and self-possessed, eautiful and kind ... you are truly a credit to your parents. We have always nought you were special and now a special man chooses you for his wife. There e black-skinned women of greater social class but he chooses you, the daughter f a parish schoolteacher and a laborer. I know it is not what you expected but it a gift. Take it. Later, after your babies are big enough, there will be time to work you still want to. Now is time to secure your future. Oui?" Her hand was on my eek and her eyes were kind.

"Oui, Maman," I mumbled.

Hubert came for dinner. Afterwards we took our walk around the grounds ith my arm tucked into his. When we were on the far side of the barn and out sight of the house he stopped.

"I will kiss you, now," he said. His lips came quickly and settled on mine like e would kiss a hand or a wall, with no warmth. He finished and looked at me. t does not please you, Mademoiselle?"

"No, I'm sorry," I said, honestly. "But it's nothing that cannot be fixed. Here, ll show you..." I leaned toward him to do the kissing and he pulled back further, expression of disgust on his face. "I'm only trying to show you what it should like."

"Show me? You dare to tell me how to kiss? I have to wonder how many men ave felt your lips that you feel qualified to teach me anything? My kiss is fine. ve never had a complaint."

He then turned and stalked off and I was left, embarrassed and ashamed at the barn with the sounds of the chickens and pigs seeming to laugh at me. hurried to catch up to him.

"Hubert," I said, trying to take his arm. "I'm sorry. I did not mean to offen you. I meant nothing." He stopped again, his color still high with anger.

"If my touch is so repulsive to you, we don't have to kiss again. And since don't know where you've been, we will come together for mating only. Once ou children are born we need never touch at all. Will you take your hand off m Mademoiselle?"

I was confused. He had flipped on me so quickly and completely. An irrationally. I removed my hand. "Well, we are not married yet, so we don't hav to touch at all if we choose, nor do we have to speak. You do not need to mak the trip here to visit if you'd rather not."

"I will court you as a proper gentleman until we marry."

"You don't even want to marry me," I said. "That's obvious."

"I do want to marry you. Despite the rumors I heard in town about yo and the dead man who tried to rob your former employer, whom you had lure into a shed with your beauty. I'll admit I was disgusted by the whole sordi affair, but you are pleasing to my eye and will make handsome babies. Your lool and intelligence almost make up for your shameless promiscuity and low-cla parents. But you will not insult me again, ever. Do you understand?"

Anger washed through me in a rush.

"How dare you?" I said. "Who do you think you are to come here and spea to me like this?"

"I am your betrothed. I asked your father for your hand and he has given to me. And he has promised you will come to your senses and be a good wife me. So get in line, Mademoiselle, and don't embarrass your poor parents, furthe They, if not you, understand what is at stake here. You are twenty-three years o and still living in their home, you are a burden to them. I am doing them a favo taking you off their hands. Don't forget that. Please give them my regards."

Instead of going inside the house he walked to his carriage stiffly, still angr A loud crack of anger spurred his poor horse to take off as if being chased. Tea burned my eyes as I went inside to find my father in the parlor.

"Papa, you promised me to him?"

My parents looked up, their faces looked caught.

"Ma belle," Papa started. "It is a good match."

"It is not a good match. It is not at all. What did you tell him about me? He just called me a whore. He spouted out the lies about Guy that I've been fighting all year. He told me I was lucky he would have me. Why didn't you tell him about what happened?"

"Mon Dieu," my mother looked at my father. "You told me he knew everything."

"I could not tell him everything or he wouldn't have come. I knew once he saw our Véronique nothing else would matter."

"But it does," I said. "It does matter what he thinks about me, Papa. He said horrible things."

"Let the blame be mine, then, not his," my father said. "For not being upfront with him. I didn't think anyone would be so foul as to spread rumors to him. I will explain when I see him. Obviously, his pride was hurt ... thinking you'd had another man. I will set him right when he returns, explain that Guy was like a brother."

"I hope he doesn't return," I said.

"Véronique!" My mother said. "Don't be so cavalier, this is too important."

"I shall be whatever I want." I turned and picked up my bag and left for Madame's house.

Chapter Twelve

spent the next week training Lisette and thinking about my options until one
day Madame Adele caught me while I was fluffing the pillows in one of the spare
bedrooms. I felt her presence and turned to find her in the doorway.

"Have you decided yet?" she asked, wringing her hands.

"I was hoping to have another couple of days," I said. "The decision affects
more than just me. My family is worried."

"Why? This is a wonderful opportunity. A once-in-a-lifetime opportunity."

I straightened and told her plainly. "When I told my mother about the
training she was not as happy for me as I had expected. She wants me to marry
Hubert Pentier more than she wants me to work. I was so angry when I left
last night but on the walk back here I could only think of my parents' faces. I
know they want only the best for me but ever since Hubert showed up, it seems
every day unearths a new layer of fear my parents hold for me. I used to be a
confident woman and now I wonder if they know something I don't. If I'm a fool
to consider living life I want instead of doing the smart thing. The safe thing."

"Nonsense," Madame said. "Who said marriage is safe? There is no part of it
that's safe. I told you how kind my first husband was, how he saved me and my
family from sure ruin?" She sat down on the bed and I followed suit. "What I
didn't tell you about was the constant fear I lived with. From how to wear my hair
to how to dress, how to speak, how to walk, how to chew my food in his presence
. I was constantly worried I would do something—anything—to displease him,
and knowing that to do so would leave me out on the street. To lose him would
be worse than never having had him in the first place."

"But you said he was kind."

"He was the kindest man. It hurt his heart that I spent our whole marriage
feeling beholden to him. Our marriage was one of gratitude, not love. I tried to
earn the right to be his wife. He truly only wanted a wife to love him. But he
was the one with the power, you see? No matter how much I liked him I could
never forget that without him I was nothing. And so I could never truly love him
as a wife should love her husband. He deserved to be loved," she said that last
statement, wistfully as if seeing him standing before her.

"My parents love each other deeply so I don't understand why they don't want the same for me," I said.

She sighed. "Because they are parents and you are their precious baby. Your mother speaks of you with the love sitting on her like rouge on her cheeks obvious for anyone to see. You are her heart. She wants her heart to be safe. And in this world, marriage is a much safer prospect than work, for any woman. It's an elevation in society. I can understand why she would want it for you."

Madame stood and brushed her skirt down, her face serious and sad.

"But what do you think? Madame, what do you advise?"

She looked at me, shamefaced. "I advise you to toughen up, Véronique. I take off my employer cloak and suddenly see you as a daughter and I feel your mother's fear for you because you are too sweet. Too kind. You do not see that I am obviously concerned only with my own convenience."

"Madame, what do you mean?"

She turned to walk to the door, almost angry in stride, but then turned back and glared at me. "For goodness' sake, Véronique, have you not heard a word I've said. I am a selfish woman. I have lived my life trying to be good enough for this society that chews women up and spits them out. It would be a feather in my cap to have a staff member train at the du Barry household. It would elevate *me*. It would make me and my husband the most impressive household in Burgundy. Do you hear me, Véronique? Your labor would benefit *us*.

"I tell you to go work because it serves me, not for your benefit. Lissette has neither your talent nor intelligence; it would be a miracle if she lasted a week at a place like that. But you, you could do it and I would get all the credit. Because I am still trying to be good enough. Even after marrying two well-respected men. Still trying!" Her eyes glinted suddenly with the threat of tears. "Marriage is neither safe nor easy but at least you shall never be without a roof over your head or a man to fight for your honor. Don't take the job. Listen to your mother. She loves you and wants only the best for you. Marry your suitor, at least then you will never be hungry. I will send Lissette instead, she has no suitor nor prospect to lose."

**

spent the rest of the week working hard. But I also found quiet times when was cleaning a bedroom or sweeping the stone ground behind the house to think. Thinking about my choices and lack of them. Thinking about my father and how much I respected and loved both my parents. Thinking about the vice I felt slowly tightening around my heart as my future sat before me, the cost of its embrace being all that I knew and held dear.

Daughters of good families did as they were told. I'd been a good daughter all my life and I didn't want to change now. But I knew with certainty that marriage to Hubert would kill my soul.

"*You are too good for this place,*" Guy had said.

I didn't believe I was too good for Burgundy. But I did now see that there was no place left for me in my hometown. Perhaps, soon, there'd be no place for me even in my own family with the decision I was making. My father would surely disown me.

That Sunday I went home earlier than usual. I had rolled and packed my first dress into a large cloth bag by the time my mother's diminutive figure lit the bedroom doorway.

"You came through so quickly, do you not say hello to your mother these days?" She stopped when she noticed me pushing clothes into the bag. I didn't keep much at Madame's and I wanted more changes.

"What are you doing?"

"I must finish quickly. Madame sent me in the carriage so I wouldn't have to walk back with all my bags with me. I mustn't keep the driver waiting."

"What?" she rushed to the front window and looked down at the carriage that had brought me. "Véronique!" My mother came forward to me, her face a mask of panic. I hated that she looked so frightened, but it couldn't be helped.

My father was in the doorway now, his face, also, almost awash of emotion as numb.

"Why is the Madame's carriage out front? What is happening?" I didn't respond. "Véronique, daughter, stop what you are doing this instant. Stop and speak to us. We are your parents, you will respect us!"

His raised voice didn't stop me but the slight sob in his tone did. I stopped and looked at them, these two people who were my life.

"I cannot marry Hubert," I said. "I'm sorry. I know you want what's best for me, but he is not it. I have an opportunity to explore new things and I must take it."

"New things?" my mother asked. "You are still cleaning houses, only now you will be doing it for a wealthier white woman, what is the difference? This is marriage to an upper-class man—a marriage that will open doors for you that we never could."

"Maman, Papa ... all my life you've taught me to fear nothing and yet now you tell me to plan my entire future based on nothing but fear. Now, when I need to be bravest, you hobble me with your fear for me. I see the panic in your face and it frightens me more than any of the choices before me. Do you not believe in me, after all?"

"No," my mother stepped forward, her face softening. "No, Chère, it is not you we doubt. It's this world. You are beautiful and young in a town that barely sees you. Half of the people in Burgundy feel black people should be enslaved and they resent your very presence. They bristle when they find out you can read and write. We know, your father and I, that it's been difficult being so alone here. Maybe we sheltered you too much. You and Guy, we have parented you wrong if we failed to teach you the realities in life."

"You taught me the realities, Maman, but you also taught me to be brave in the face of them. How can the two of you who love each other so much ask me to accept less? Haven't you always told me love can conquer anything? It hasn't been easy for the two of you. I've seen how people treat you. I've seen how hard you've fought just to be part of this town. Aren't the two of you proof that with the right person by your side you can survive anything? Maman, you yourself told me that when you love a man you will take all his pain on yourself, if you can. I want to marry the man I love that much. I want him to love me that much."

"Oh, now you will use our relationship against us to prove your case? Our love is rare, most people don't get half as much."

"Is that what I should settle for then, Maman, half as much? You told me that it wouldn't have helped Guy for me to destroy myself for love of him; that to do so would only add to his pain and dishonor him. Are you asking me now to destroy myself by settling for what you want for me? Marriage to Hubert will kill me. He will breed me and then ignore me like a farm animal. Can't you understand, I'm trying to save myself and in doing so, I will save your dignity all the same. I honor you by honoring myself."

My mother grew quiet, and I felt a little guilty, using her own words against her, though Papa continued. "I will never deny that loving your mother has saved my life," he tried. "But you can grow into love, also. Love can be a choice."

I looked away from my mother's still face to my father's worried one. "The way Hubert spoke to me ... I have plenty of reason to doubt he would ever choose to love me that way. I will always be the farm girl he saved. I don't want to be beholden to that. I don't want to be like Madame, a woman so desperate for social acceptance she has to rely on her servant to earn her a little more respect. I don't want to be a fancy woman defined by materialism and things. I want love. I want happiness. I want to know my worth. I want a little house on a river where I can sew and make beautiful things with my own two hands. I want a simple life, and when I marry, if I marry, I want it to be with a man I choose."

I went back to pushing the rest of my clothes into the bag, ignoring the tears that streaked my mother's cheeks. I couldn't bear to see them. At the sound of a neighing horse I looked out the window and saw Hubert climbing down from his carriage.

By the time I opened the front door he was there, looking confused. He noticed the large bag I carried. "What is this? Who is that driver for?" he asked. There was no way to do it but to do it.

"I offer my sincerest apologies, Monsieur Pentier. I cannot marry you and my decision is final. Please do not blame my parents, they encouraged me to accept your hand. They have a great deal of respect for you. This is my decision and my decision alone."

These were big words coming from a woman who was, technically, her father's property. This was the moment when my father could, by rights, take me by the arm and steer me back inside the house. He could, legally, confine me and call for a priest to come to the home to marry me to Hubert. I really only held as much choice over who I wed as my father would allow.

I waited for Papa to stop me. So did Hubert. As the moment stretched and it became evident my father wouldn't step forward, my heart filled with a lightness I'd never known as the burden lifted. The feeling of relief that flooded me was so expansive, it even reached Hubert who, realizing my father didn't intend to force me, lost all semblance of the gentleman.

His face changed from stunned to angry to ugly. "How dare you treat me like this? You are lucky I ever even considered marrying a woman like you."

"And you are lucky I said no. It would not have ended well, Monsieur. I wish you the best."

I walked away from him towards the carriage.

"You will never marry," Hubert called after me. "You have shamed your parents. You will be alone forever and you will die alone! And you will deserve it you ungrateful woman!"

The driver had stepped down and had put my bag inside and was climbing back up front when I stopped. I couldn't tell you what stopped me. A touch of the fear I claimed not to have held me in that moment, as all I knew and loved was behind me. And then I felt a hand on my shoulder. I turned to see my mother standing there, my father just behind, faces awash in tears.

"Maman, Papa, please don't be disappointed in me. Please forgive me. I'm sorry. I'm so sorry." I hated that I sounded like a little girl but that was how I felt.

My mother touched my cheek. "My love, you are the courageous woman we raised." She glanced at my papa. "Look at her, so brave and bold. This is the girl we raised, is it not? You will go, my Chère. And you will do what you need to do in the way you need to do it. And we will always love you."

My father's face showed he was out of words. Instead, he reached up and cupped my head. Together the three of us stood for a long moment and then pulled away. I smiled through my tears and climbed into the back of the carriage. I looked back once to see them—my parents holding each other and the man would have married looking rigid and confused—and then I sat back and stared straight ahead.

As the driver carried me away I willed myself to be as brave as I wanted to be.

I didn't know what life in the household of the Madame du Barry would be like. I didn't know what the future had in store for me. But as the carriage rode away from my family home I slowly began to smile through my tears.

My mother had told me that no one comes to our small town and no one ever leaves. I would be the first, then.

I had made my first step on my own.

Pray God it was the right decision...

VÉRONIQUE'S JOURNEY

Fin

About this Title
Véronique's Journey

by

Patti Flinn

Up until recently there was little said about the presence of black people in Europe throughout history. At least, very little I was taught here in the U.S. But as an African American Francophile and lover of beautiful historical dramas, once I began to research, I became determined to develop a sweeping saga featuring a French person of African descent.

The fictional character introduced in this novella, Véronique Clair, leaves her rural home in Burgundy the summer of 1788 to journey across the country to enter a world of luxury and extravagance at the Chateau du Barry in Louveciennes, France.

Véronique's story doesn't end with **Véronique's Journey.**

This novella is the parallel story to an upcoming series set in Louveciennes, a stone's throw from the Palace of Versailles, during the reign of King Louis XVI. The series is inspired by a very real person in history and Véronique will become a pivotal influence on that person's life and actions during the French Revolution.

I would love for you to continue with Véronique on this journey back to 18th century, France.

Subscribe at http://gildedorangebooks.com to be notified of the upcoming series.

Discussion Questions
Véronique's Journey

by
Patti Flinn

1. What do you think Véronique's Clair's decision?

1. What, if any, alternatives might Véronique have taken?

1. This story takes place in a little town in Burgundy, France in 1788. Based on what is happening during the U.S. during this time period, how did that influence your understanding or belief of the situation on mainland France for black people?

1. As the parents of a daughter during this time, how well do you think Véronique's parents prepared her for the real world?

1. Do you think Véronique should have agreed to marry Guy?

1. Was Véronique's father's decision to only look for a black husband harm her? Was he being selfish?

1. In a society where work was less of an occupation and more of the identity of the individual, is it understandable why the loss of his job impacted Guy in such an extreme manner?

1. Hubert made it clear Véronique was lucky to have him. Why do you think, feeling the way he did about her and her social status, he considered marrying her in the first place?

1. Was Madame Martin kind or self-serving? What did her continued concern about social status suggest about the standards of the time?

1. With all that was going on in the world, what are your hopes for Véronique and are her dreams achievable?

CPSIA information can be obtained
at www.ICGtesting.com
Printed in the USA
LVHW080058190822
726215LV00012B/355

9 798986 060019